ALIEN ADVENTURE
IT'S OK!
WE'RE GOING TO SAVE THE PLANET!

FOR THOMAS

FOR PHILIPPA

Scholastic Children's Books
An imprint of Scholastic Ltd
Euston House, 24 Eversholt Street, London, NW1 1DB, UK
Registered office: Westfield Road, Southam, Warwickshire, CV47 0RA
SCHOLASTIC and associated logos are trademarks and/or
registered trademarks of Scholastic Inc.

First published in the UK by Scholastic Ltd, 2016

Text and illustrations copyright © Andrew Judge and Chris Judge, 2016

The right of Andrew Judge and Chris Judge to be identified as the authors of this work has been asserted by them.

ISBN 978 1407 15809 9

A CIP catalogue record for this book
is available from the British Library.

Printed by CPI Group (UK) Ltd, Croydon, CR0 4YY
Papers used by Scholastic Children's Books are made
from wood grown in sustainable forests.

3 5 7 9 10 8 6 4 2

www.scholastic.co.uk

CREATE YOUR OWN

ALIEN ADVENTURE

IT'S OK!
WE'RE GOING TO SAVE THE PLANET!

ANDREW JUDGE & CHRIS JUDGE

SCHOLASTIC

STOP!

I know what you are thinking.

You want to flick ahead to the exciting bits.

Like the **ESCAPE FROM THE ALIEN ZOO** on page 95 and the **EPIC SPACE BATTLE** on page 106.

I bet you do!

But first we have to get the boring bits out of the way.

Only joking! This is a book about **ALIENS**! It's **ALL** exciting.

What's also great about this book is that **YOU** get to join in. So grab a pen or a pencil and draw some **CRATERS** on the moon and a **SOLAR PANEL** on the space station! You can also draw some stars if you like.

You don't need to draw any of the missing bits on
this spaceship though.

It's not unfinished.

IT'S CRASHING!

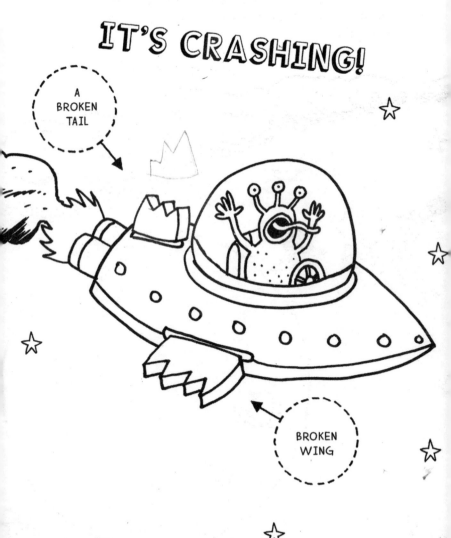

A
BROKEN
TAIL

BROKEN
WING

7

Meet B'ob. He's one of the heroes in this story.
Say hello to the reader, B'ob.

"⫽⟋⟍⸴⁊⦙ ⌷⊣�482⸴ ⅃⁊ⅲⅈⅈ⫽" says B'ob.

OK. So maybe now is a bad time.
We'll come back later.

Now where was I? Ah, yes! **DOODLES**. This isn't just a story about aliens. It's also filled with Doodles. What's a Doodle, you ask?*

This is a Doodle. Daisy Doodle to be precise. She is the other hero of the story.

IT'S VERY NICE TO MEET YOU!

*You didn't ask? Oh. Well, now you know anyway.

Daisy and her friends live in Doodletown. It is a very nice town, as you can see, except for one **SMALL** problem. Everything is half drawn with bits and pieces missing!

*Can you draw my face please?

The Doodles are going to need **YOUR** help. So grab a pen or a pencil and finish the Doodles on this page.

So, are you ready to start?

YES

NO*

LET'S BEGIN!

*Did you tick NO? Really? Oh. Turn to page 128.

CHAPTER ONE

SCHOOL!

It is Thursday morning and Daisy Doodle is on her way to school. It is a lovely sunny day. Or maybe it isn't because **THE WEATHER ISN'T DRAWN YET**. Maybe the sun is shining or maybe there is a **HUGE** thunder and lightning storm. **YOU** decide, because that's the way this book works!

DRAW SOME WEATHER HERE

So what's it to be? Sunshine or rain? Daisy is hoping that it is sunny, because she has forgotten her coat.

Daisy arrives at school in a good mood. Or soaking wet. It really depends on what you drew.

She spots her best friend Donny outside the school gates. Donny gives her a big wave and runs over.

"Hey, Daisy. Did you see that movie about the alien invasion last night? It was cool!"

Daisy nods. "Yes, but why do they always make the aliens the baddies? Some of them must be nice. I bet I could make friends with an alien if it came to visit Doodletown."

Donny laughs. "An alien in Doodletown? That's not likely to happen, is it?"

"Well," says Daisy, "if I meet one, I'll let you know."

Daisy and Donny wander into the playground. The bell hasn't rung yet so everyone is trying to have fun before school starts. Except they have forgotten to bring things to play with.

Look at these guys trying to skip without a skipping rope. Can you draw one for them?

And these kids are playing soccer without a ball! Add one in with your pen.

The bell rings, **LINGA-LINGA-LINGA-LING!** It is time to line up for class. Miss Scribble comes out of the school to gather everyone together. But she seems to have forgotten something!

She waves her arms in front of her and stumbles around the playground. "Hello? Where is everybody?"

"It looks like she's lost her glasses again," says Daisy.

Can you draw some on her?

"Draw a **BIG MOUSTACHE** too!" says Donny.

Suddenly Miss Scribble can see.

"Ah, there you are," she says twirling her moustache. **TWIRLING HER MOUSTACHE!? WHAT THE?**

"EEEEK! Who drew this moustache on me?" she yells.

The whole class bursts out laughing. It's not every day you see your teacher with a big handlebar moustache.

"That's enough fun for now," says Miss Scribble as she erases her moustache and straightens her glasses. "Everybody line up, please."

The whole class forms a line while Miss Scribble counts them. "Twenty-one, twenty-two. Twenty-two? We are one short. Where is Undrawn John?"

"I'm here," says a voice. "I'm just not drawn yet."

LOOK! IT'S UNDRAWN JOHN!

Miss Scribble sighs. "Can somebody please draw Undrawn John?"

Do you want to have a go?

"Follow me," says Miss Scribble at last as she leads the class to the school entrance.

But look! Someone has erased the door while Miss Scribble wasn't looking.

"This is **RIDICULOUS**!" says Miss Scribble in annoyance. "The door is gone again! Can anybody help?"

ENTRANCE

QUICK! You had better draw a door before Daisy and her class get into more trouble.

Finally the school yard is empty. Which is a pity because the very next moment something **UNBELIEVABLE** happens.

AN ALIEN SPACESHIP FALLS FROM THE SKY!

Imagine! The one thing Daisy wanted to see and she just missed it by **ONE PAGE!**

The spaceship shoots across the sky, billowing smoke from its tail. Or at least it will be billowing smoke when you draw some billowing smoke.

DRAW LOTS OF SMOKE

Exciting stuff, eh?

Meanwhile, inside, Miss Scribble is droning on about space and planets and stars. That might sound a bit **INTERESTING** to you, but Miss Scribble has a way of making the most **EXCITING** thing in the universe sound boring. Do you know any teachers like that?

No? Well, you are one of the lucky ones, I guess.

PLANET SCRATCHPAD

SMILE ISLAND

Miss Scribble is explaining that some planets are made out of rocks and some are made out of gas. See what I mean? **EXCITING**. Not.

"Our Planet Scratchpad is just the right distance from the sun," she continues. "It is not too hot and not too cold. It is just the right temperature to allow us to live here. Like Goldilocks's porridge. Except it's not porridge. It's a planet. I hope you are taking notes."

Daisy is one of the few students still awake. "What sort of planets do aliens come from, Miss?"

Miss Scribble pauses mid-drone. "Daisy Doodle, how many times do I have to tell you? Aliens **DON'T** exist! Stop asking silly questions."

"OK," says Daisy. "But what is that looking in the window then?"

Miss Scribble **SCREAMS!**

Because there is an **ALIEN** looking in the window!

DRAW A SCREAM

CHAPTER TWO

CHASE!

Everybody stares at the window. The alien stares back. "**EEEEK!**" says Miss Scribble helpfully.

The whole class leaps to their feet, knocking over chairs and desks, and races outside. Daisy and Penny are the fastest but even they are not quick enough to catch the alien. There is no sign of it in the yard.

Daisy's heart sinks. "We missed it!"

Penny says, "Look! A clue!" There on the ground are some strangely shaped muddy footprints.

Daisy's eyes widen. "Woah! It **WAS** an alien!"

The footprints lead from the classroom window out across the school yard.

START DRAWING SOME FOOTPRINTS HERE

There are three places the alien could have gone. It's up to you to decide. Where do the footprints lead?

If the footprints lead here then turn to page 26 to continue.

If the footprints lead here then turn to page 32.

Or maybe they lead here? Go to page 38.

HOLD IT!

Where do you think you are going? You can't just wander out of school without permission. That's **CRAZY!**

You had better go and get a permission slip.

Fold down the corner of the page so that you will remember where you are and then go to the Principal's office on page 127.

FOLD DOWN THE CORNER

TICK! TICK! TICK!

Good. You're back.
Did you get the permission slip?

 YES Then turn the page and continue.

 NO What are you still doing here?
Go back to page 127.

Daisy follows the footprints across the playground and out on to Inky Avenue. It is a busy town, the **PERFECT PLACE** to hide an alien.

It could be peeping over the fence. Or hiding in the doorway. What's that in the postbox? Could it be on the roof?

Decide where the alien is hiding and draw it in. Daisy **MIGHT** spot it with your help.

Daisy reaches the Doodle-town fire station and has a **GREAT IDEA**.

"If I could get up high," she says, looking upwards at the tower, "I would be able to spot the alien."

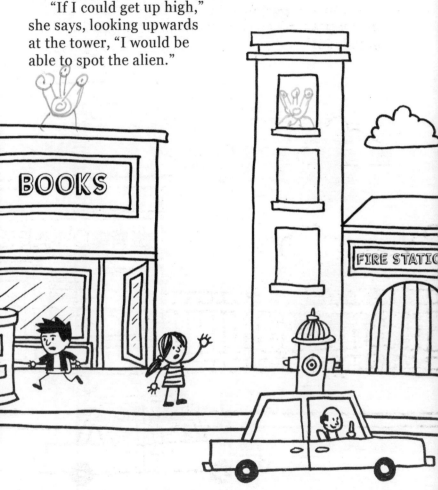

BOOKS

FIRE STATIO

Can you think of a way for her to get up the tower?
Draw something to help her.

Up ...   and up ...   and up she goes ...   until she reaches the top.

"Phew! Made it!" she says as she stops to catch her breath. Then, "Wow," as she turns around and sees the view spread out below her. She can see **ALL** of Doodletown from here. But no alien. Out at the edge of the town she notices something unusual: a large crater that was not there last Tuesday!

"Now **THAT** is interesting," says Daisy. "I think I shall go and take a look."

Turn to page 42.

DRAW SOME HOUSES

Daisy runs to the gap in the fence and is about to slip
through when Chalky the Caretaker spots her.
"Where do you think you are going?" asks Chalky.
Daisy points frantically to the gap in the fence.
"I'm chasing an alien who went this way."

"Well," says Chalky, "you need permission from
the principal to chase aliens outside school grounds."
Daisy rolls her eyes.

You had better do what he says. Fold down the corner
of the page so that you will remember where you are
and then go to the Principal's office on page 127.

Did you get the permission slip on page 127?

No? Well you had better go and get it then.
Yes? Great. Let's continue.

Daisy slips through the gap in the fence and into the woods beside the school. She stands still and listens carefully. She realizes she has never noticed all the little noises before.

A bird calls from high up in a tree. A dog barks in the distance. There is a crack of twigs from inside a bush. Something goes "**GORP**". The wind rustles the leaves.

Excuse me? Did you say "**GORP**"?

Do you know **ANYTHING** that goes "**GORP**"? I don't. It must be the alien!

Daisy takes off running as quick as she can. She races through the woods, ducking branches and jumping over logs.

Daisy reaches the river. Her way is blocked and she has no way across. She is **STUCK**.

What is she going to do?

Maybe you can draw something to help her across.

What about a **ROPE SWING?** Or a **FALLEN TREE?** I bet you can think of something good.

Once she is safely across the river Daisy heads deeper and deeper into the woods. It gets darker and darker as the trees get taller and taller. Soon she is lost.

At last she comes to a clearing.

I need to climb a **REALLY** tall tree to see where I am, thinks Daisy.

Can you help? Draw a **REALLY** tall tree for her to climb.

Daisy climbs the tree and pops her head above the canopy. She looks around to get her bearings.

She spots **SOMETHING STRANGE**. At the edge of the woods there is a giant crater. That's not **NORMAL**, is it?

"It looks like something has crashed," says Daisy, "and I'm going to find out what!"

Now turn to page 42 to find out what is going on.

Daisy races to the recycling bins to catch the alien. She arrives **JUST IN TIME** to see them being loaded on to a bin lorry. She looks around desperately for the alien but there is no sign of it.

From the corner of her eye she spots something.

"Oh my goodness! Is that the alien in the back of the lorry?"

It is! It's the alien peeping out!

DRAW THE ALIEN HERE

DOODLETOWN RECYCLING

YOUR PAPER.
YOU'RE PAPER.

Daisy runs towards the alien. But the bin man **BLOCKS** her way.

"What are you doing here?" he says. "It's dangerous to run behind a bin lorry."

Daisy points to the back of the lorry. "But there is an alien in there."

"Is that a fact?" says the bin man. "Well, your alien might have permission to be here, but **YOU** don't."

FOLD THE CORNER OF THE PAGE

DRAW THE ALIEN HERE

He's right. Daisy needs **PERMISSION** to leave the school grounds. Fold down the corner of the page so that you will remember where you are and then go to the Principal's office on page 127.

Did you get the permission slip on page 127?

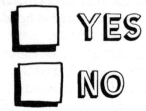 YES

NO

No? Back to page 127 then.
Yes? OK. Let's keep going.

By the time Daisy gets back from the Principal's office with the permission slip, the lorry is **GONE**. She has no way of catching up.

Or does she?

"I need a bike or a scooter to catch the lorry," she says.

Great idea! Can you draw her something to ride? **QUICK!** She needs to catch the lorry!

DRAW A BIKE

OR A SCOOTER

Daisy races after the lorry. She pedals (or scoots) as fast as she can but it is **IMPOSSIBLE** to catch. She realizes that the bin lorry is heading to the Doodletown Recycling Centre.

She sets off as fast as she can, but when she gets to the centre there is still **NO SIGN** of the lorry. There is a **HUGE** pile of cardboard boxes though. She scrambles up the huge heap until she reaches the very top. She catches her breath and looks around.

There, in the distance, she spots something **MYSTERIOUS** and **CRATER-ISH**.

"That looks like a **MYSTERIOUS CRATER**!" she says. "I think I shall check it out!"

What will happen next? Turn to page 42 to find out!

CHAPTER THREE

SPACESHIP!

Daisy arrives at the crater. She peers over the edge and sees a **CRASHED SPACESHIP!**

AWESOME!

The spaceship, I mean. Not the crashed bit. That's not awesome. That's bad.

This must be how the alien got here! Maybe it is nearby.

Daisy creeps closer. The spaceship looks like it is badly damaged. There is a big gash along the side where it has been ripped open in the crash.

You need to rip the page along the line.

Daisy decides to peep inside. Maybe the alien is hiding in there. Would you be brave enough to do that?

I wouldn't, **NO WAY!**

Daisy peers inside the damaged spaceship. It is very dark and she can't see much.

If only I had a torch, she thinks.

There's a good idea. Draw her a torch so she can see inside.

CLICK!
The torch turns on and...

"Excuse me," says Daisy, "but what did you say?"

"דדדדדﬡﬡﬧ," says the alien.

"That's what I thought," says Daisy, stroking her chin and looking thoughtful.

The alien looks at her with big sad eyes (three of them).

"ﬡﬧﬡﬡ ﬠﬠﬡﬡﬡ ﬩ﬠﬥﬦﬦﬦ ﬡﬦﬦ?" it says.

"We need to figure out way to understand each other," says Daisy.

DRAW SOME LOOSE WIRES

DRAW A BROKEN WINDOW

DRAW A CRACK IN THE FLOOR

The alien pulls a strange device out of his pocket. I know. He's not even wearing any clothes. Weird, huh? He hands the device to Daisy. It has "**TRANSLATOR**" written on it.

I bet you are thinking "Could this be a alien language translator?"

Yes. Yes, it is. Well done.

This is how it works. You fill in all the letters of the alphabet and Daisy will be able to translate the alien language. Cool, huh?

47

Good job! Now let's see if the translator is working.
"ᑕᖀ ᑕᗡ ᐃᐧ☰ᓘᑕᐧᐧᓯ ᔐᒑᑕ?," says the alien.
Daisy presses the ON button.

BLIP!

"Can you understand me?," says the alien. Wow!
It works! Isn't technology **GREAT**!

The alien is **SO EXCITED** that he bursts into tears and starts talking without taking a breath.

"MY NAME IS B'OBSTRRRK(FLN)TP AND I'M HUNGRY AND I'M LOST AND I DON'T KNOW WHERE I AM AND I'M HUNGRY AND I WANT TO GO HOME AND I'M HUNGRY AND I NEED HELP!"

(Big breath!)

"AND I'M HUNGRY," he says finally.

"It's OK, B'obstrrrk(fln)tp, I'll help you," says Daisy. "But do you mind if I call you B'ob?"

B'ob is delighted. "Not at all," he says. "What's your name?"

"It's Daisy," says Daisy.

"What a weird name," says B'ob. "But I like it."

DRAW SOME TEARS

Poor B'ob is hungry. Did he mention that?
  "First things first," says Daisy. "Let's get you something to eat."

What do you think an alien would like to eat?
  Oh yeah?
  Let's draw it for him then.

DRAW YOUR FAVOURITE FOOD

Now that B'ob has eaten your delicious pizza/sausages/carrots/chocolate cake (or whatever you drew) he is feeling much better.

"OK," says Daisy. "Time to fix this spaceship."

They are going to need some tools. You can help by drawing some.

There was a lot of damage in the crash. Daisy figures out that they need to reconnect the equipment and make sure everything is working first.

Draw some wires to join up the connectors. Different colours would help. Just make sure **THEY DO NOT CROSS**.

Connect the two **RED** wires.

Connect the two **BLUE** wires.

Connect the two **YELLOW** wires.

RED

BLUE

YELLOW

When the rewiring is finished Daisy checks it carefully. "It looks good! Let's hope it works."

The ship is nearly ready for take-off. Only one more thing needs to be done.

"We need to fix the broken wings," says Daisy. "Do you have any sticky tape?"

If you do, then go back to page 43 and tape the page. But don't worry if you don't have any sticky tape. Just keep the pages closed very tightly when the spaceship takes off.

We're ready to start the neutron engine. How fast can you draw a spiral? Faster than the speed of light, I hope, because you need to get this engine spinning!

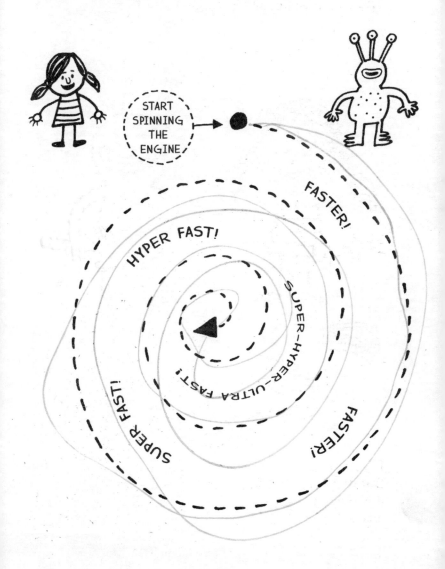

START SPINNING THE ENGINE

FASTER!

HYPER FAST!

SUPER-HYPER-ULTRA FAST!

SUPER FAST!

FASTER!

Wow! You sure are fast on the draw! The engine is spinning **SUPER-HYPER-ULTRA-FAST!**

"Cool," says Daisy, watching as the engine glows brighter and brighter.

"**POIT**," says the engine with a sudden flash.

B'ob points excitedly. "Look at that! We just made a spinning pulsar star."

The engine is powered up. We're ready to **ROCK!**
Are you ready to press the launch button?

5...

4...

3...

2...

1... GO!

The whole spaceship rattles and shakes as the engines roar. The ship prepares for launch. Daisy and B'ob are holding on as tightly as they can to their seats.

"**WAHOOO**!" says B'ob.

Suddenly Daisy realizes they forgot to fix the steering wheel. "Oh no! We've no way of steering this thing!"

BLAST OFF!

The spaceship **LEAPS** off the ground and rockets skyward, leaving a huge trail of smoke.

DRAW LOTS OF FLAMES

DRAW SMOKE

MORE SMOKE

CHAPTER FOUR
SPACE

The spaceship **SHOOTS** into orbit.

"This is cool," says Daisy. "Where to next?"

"Home," says B'ob as he sets the satnav, "if you'd like to visit?"

TURN LEFT IN 384 THOUSAND KM

The ship accelerates away from Planet Scratchpad and out into space. Daisy and B'ob look out the window. There goes the moon!

"I thought there would be more craters," says Daisy.

She's right. It looks very blank. Draw in some craters.

The satnav flashes a warning as they enter an asteroid field.

"Hang on," says B'ob, holding the steering wheel tightly. "This could be rough."

DRAW LOTS AND LOTS OF ASTEROIDS

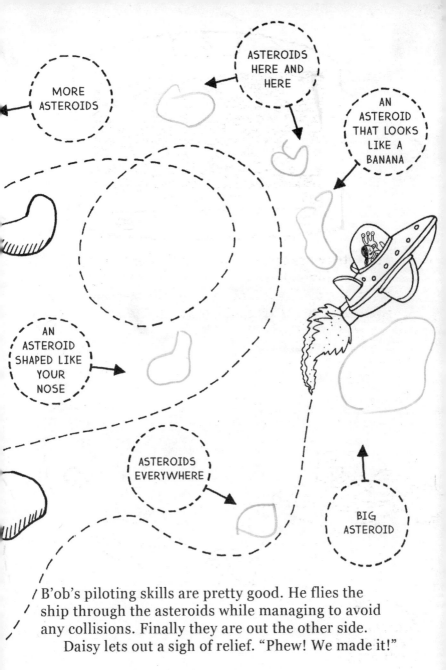

B'ob's piloting skills are pretty good. He flies the ship through the asteroids while managing to avoid any collisions. Finally they are out the other side.

Daisy lets out a sigh of relief. "Phew! We made it!"

B'ob and Daisy catch their breath while they study the star map.

"How do you plan to get home?" Daisy asks B'ob. "It looks like a long way."

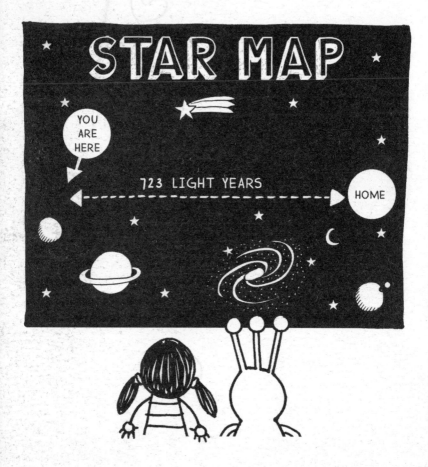

B'ob gives her a wink with two of his eyes. "That's easy! We use the warp engine to fold space!"

on the **OTHER SIDE** of the galaxy!

YOU HAVE REACHED YOUR DESTINATION.

CHAPTER FIVE

TROUBLE!

The spaceship enters orbit around Planet Greyscale just as the fuel warning light starts flashing.

B'ob looks nervous. "We've got to land this thing. We are way low on gas."

Daisy stares at the control panel. "Hmm. Which button should we press?"

Can you help? Choose a button to press.

TURN TO PAGE 125

DO NOT PRESS THIS BUTTON*

THIS IS THE BUTTON YOU SHOULD PRESS!

AUTOPILOT

CRASH

EXPLODE

LAND

*What? You pressed the **EXPLODE** button? Are you crazy?
Turn to page 126.

You pressed the **LAND** button. Good choice!

The autopilot takes over and guides the spaceship down towards the surface of the planet while Daisy looks out the window.

She notices something odd. "Everything is grey!"

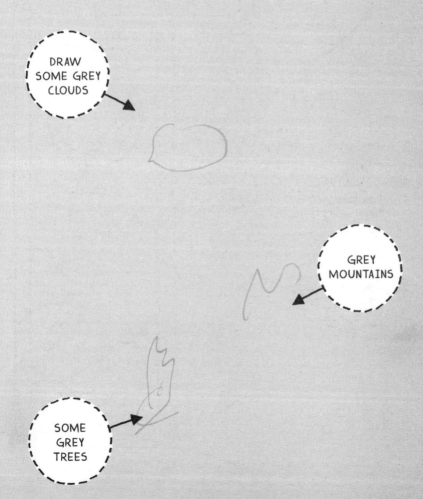

DRAW SOME GREY CLOUDS

GREY MOUNTAINS

SOME GREY TREES

They fly over grey oceans, grey beaches, grey roads and grey fields.

"Look! There's my house." B'ob points out the window.

The spaceship lands and B'ob opens the door. Just as Daisy is climbing out, a small alien runs out of the house.

"Uh-oh! It's my little sister," says B'ob from the corner of his mouth.

B'ob's sister marches up to him. "You are in **SO** much trouble!"

Suddenly an **ENORMOUS, SCARY** alien bursts from the house!

The monster roars with anger.

"B'OBSTRRRK(FLN)TPK!!"

It lunges at B'ob and ...

... picks him up to give him a **BIG HUG**.

"Thank goodness you are OK," it says. "Don't you ever take my spaceship again without permission."

B'ob looks embarrassed. "Sorry, Mum."

Daisy is invited to stay for dinner.

Unfortunately dinner doesn't look too appetizing. It's grey and dull.

Daisy pokes at the food on her plate. "I think this would look much tastier if it had some colour."

Can you add some colour to the food on the table?

B'ob's mum is impressed by your work. "Oh my! These colours are lovely. I had forgotten how much I love colour."

She stares wistfully out of the window.

"I remember a time when **EVERYTHING** was colourful. That was before the President took over and made everything grey."

Have you heard about the President before? No?

You're lucky! Wait till you meet him...

"I wonder," says Mum to herself. "I think I may still have some old colourful things somewhere upstairs..."

Later that evening when Daisy and B'ob have finished dinner (or at least tasted some of it out of **GOOD MANNERS**) they decide to go exploring.

"Can I bring Daisy into town?" B'ob asks his mum. Mum looks sternly at both of them. "Well all right. But be home by twenty o'clock."

B'ob and Daisy go out to **EXPLORE** the town.
Everything is unfinished, just like at home.
  Except it's worse than that.
  It's **GREY** and **BORING**!
  Even the weird fruit on the tree is grey.

They walk further into town where things get even greyer. Daisy begins to feel sorry for everyone. "They all look so unhappy."

"You're right." B'ob looks around thoughtfully. "I never really noticed before."

As Daisy and B'ob walk through town they notice posters on every wall.

Daisy points to one of the posters. "Who is that guy?"

"That's the President," says B'ob. "He's the one who banned all colour around here."

Daisy gives B'ob a big grin. "Well, maybe we should colour **HIM** then."

Do you want to give it a go?
Go on, I **DARE** you! Colour the poster in!

YOUR
PRESIDENT
LIKES YOU

TO DO WHAT HE TELLS YOU.

Have you finished colouring in the poster?

NO? Hurry up! We need to get on with the story.

YES? Excellent! Let's continue.

The poster looks great now. Good job! Daisy and B'ob step back to admire your handiwork. They do not notice someone standing right beside them.

UH-OH! It's the **SHERIFF**. And he does **NOT** look impressed!

Daisy and B'ob jump as he lets out a roar.
"WHAT'S GOING ON HERE? DID YOU DRAW ON THAT POSTER?"

The Sheriff is really annoyed. "Who gave you permission to be here?"

Daisy does some fast thinking. She remembers the **PERMISSION SLIP** you tore out of the book earlier! Do you still have it? Quickly, go and get it so that Daisy can show it to the Sheriff.

Daisy hands the permission slip to the Sheriff. He stares at it closely. He stares at Daisy. He stares back at the slip in confusion.

"What is this?" he asks. "Where are you from? Are you an alien?"

Before Daisy can answer, the Sheriff makes his decision. "You are both in **BIG TROUBLE**. I'm taking you to see the President."

The Sheriff takes Daisy and B'ob to the President's office. Guess who they meet there?

That's right, the President. Surprised? Well, you shouldn't be because I told you he would be appearing soon.

He looks very annoyed. "Who are you? Any why were you drawing on my lovely posters?" He glares at them both over his big show-off desk.

Look at him. He thinks he is great.

Daisy is **NOT** impressed by him one little bit. She doesn't like being bossed around. "I'm Daisy. I'm from a planet where we draw on everything."

The President is not happy with her answer. "Is that so? And you think that gives you the right to colour my poster?"

Daisy looks the President straight in the eye. "I thought it could do with some cheering up."

The President thumps the desk. "Nonsense!" he says. "We like things the way they are. One shade of grey is exciting enough for us, thank you very much."

The President drones on and on about colour and grey and blah and blah.

Daisy's mind begins to wander. This guy is **SO** boring, she thinks.

She's right. He doesn't even LOOK like a president! I mean, **WHERE'S HIS CROWN**? Let's turn the page and do something about that.

Do your best to make him look **RIDICULOUS**!
Draw a ludicrous **CROWN** and some crazy
EYELASHES. What about a huge **MOUSTACHE**
or some lovely red **LIPSTICK**?
   ANYTHING that makes him look silly!

Well done! The President looks really silly now.
And REALLY annoyed. He screams and shouts and
says things like:

"OUTRAGEOUS!"

and

"HOW DARE YOU!"

What a doofus.

Daisy, B'ob and the Sheriff can't help but laugh.

The President roars at the Sheriff, "Take them
away! Lock them in the zoo!"

The Sheriff tries to stop sniggering as he marches
them away. He puts them in a van and locks the
door.

This doesn't look too good...

CHAPTER SIX

ZOO!

Daisy and B'ob arrive at the zoo, which is where the aliens go on Sundays to stare at weird-looking creatures, like **DAISY**!

Remember: if you visited Planet Greyscale you would be the weird-looking alien too!

The Sheriff marches them through the entrance.

They pass a cage with a **BLORTHAK TROON** in it.
As I'm sure you know, a Blorthak Troon is a large,
monstrous creature with **TEN ARMS**. It is very hairy
and fearsome with a mouth full of sharp teeth, but it
is in fact quite cuddly and has a lovely smile.

Do your best drawing of a Blorthak Troon in the cage.

BLORTHAK TROON

Daisy is impressed with the Blorthak Troon. "Woah!
She would be a good goalkeeper for our soccer team."

Daisy and B'ob are locked in enclosures next to two other creatures.

The first is a **WINDLE**, which is a large blob with four eyes, two wobbly ears and a nice haircut. It has a trunk that it uses to suck up small insects.

The second is a **PLOMP**, a tiny creature the size of a dot. It is so tiny that you can barely see its **FORTY LEGS** and **FORTY ARMS**. It also likes to wear tiny hats.

DRAW A WINDLE

DRAW A PLOMP

PLOMP

WINDLE

Daisy is feeling very sorry for herself. "What are we going to do, B'ob? This adventure isn't going so well."

B'ob has no answer. He is too busy worrying what his mum will say when she finds out he has been put in the zoo.

What would your mother say if you were locked in a zoo?

 "Well done, I am very proud of you."

 "Why am I not surprised?"

I bet you are thinking things can't get much worse.
WRONG!
Because here comes ...

... the President.

He is very smug and full of himself. "You are not so clever now, eh, Doodle?"

DAISY

"I didn't mean any harm," says Daisy.

"That's not good enough," says the President. "I'm going to teach you a lesson."

What a meany.

He shows Daisy his p[...]
more and more horrifie[...]

THE PRESID[...]
excellent PL[...]

PLANET
GREYSCALE

PLANET
SCRATCHPAD

My Invasion fleet

The President is delighted with himself. "I am going to invade your home planet with my fleet of 573 spaceships* and make everything **GREY**!"
   OH NO!

*What do you mean you can't see 573 spaceships? You're supposed to draw them!

ESCAPE!

After the President has gone Daisy sits down to think. This is **PRETTY BAD**! What is she going to do?

Just then a voice says, "I could help if you like."

Daisy spins around. "Undrawn John! Where did you come from?"

IT'S UNDRAWN JOHN!

"I've been with you all the time," says John. "I just wasn't drawn."

Well! Isn't **THAT** a nice surprise? John deserves to be **DRAWN** for that, don't you think?

Undrawn John has a plan. He reaches into his pocket and takes out ...

HIS INVISIBLE PENCIL!

Have you ever seen an invisible pencil? No? Me neither. John holds up his invisible pencil (at least, Daisy thinks he does).

"It's not very good for drawing," he says, "but it's great for undrawing."

TEAR THIS
PIECE
OF THE
PAGE OUT

Carefully he draws a shape on the wall of the cage.

Daisy watches in **AMAZEMENT** as the side of the cage **DISAPPEARS**. "Wow! I can't believe what I'm not seeing."

Daisy and Undrawn John jump from the cage and run to free B'ob.

But they are quickly spotted by the Sheriff and the Zoo Attendant. Time to get out of here!

TEAR THIS
BIT OF
THE PAGE
OUT

They run through the zoo looking for a way to
ESCAPE.

Which way should they go?

To the exit door? Turn to page 96.

To the big balloon in the sky? Turn to page 100.

So you decided to escape through the **EXIT** door?

The **EXIT** leads to a small room with a platform and a control panel. It's a **TELEPORTER!**

"Great! We can teleport out of here," says B'ob.

There are **THREE** buttons. Which will you press?

Whoops! It looks like you pressed the wrong button. You've **SWAPPED** everybody's heads! "What the..." says Daisy/B'ob/Undrawn John.

You had better try again.

Oh dear. You are not very good at working a teleporter, are you?

Daisy looks down. "Where's the rest of me?"

"Urg! My head is where my feet should be," says Undrawn John.

Try again!

FINALLY, you pressed the correct button. The teleporter works properly.

"At last," says Daisy. "Let's get out of here."

Now turn to page 104.

Daisy, B'ob and Undrawn John run to the balloon and grab hold just as it **TAKES OFF**.

But it isn't a **BALLOON**! It's a

GASEOUS SPRONG!

Daisy, B'ob and Undrawn John cling on tightly as they float higher and higher.

The **GASEOUS SPRONG** releases some stinky gas!

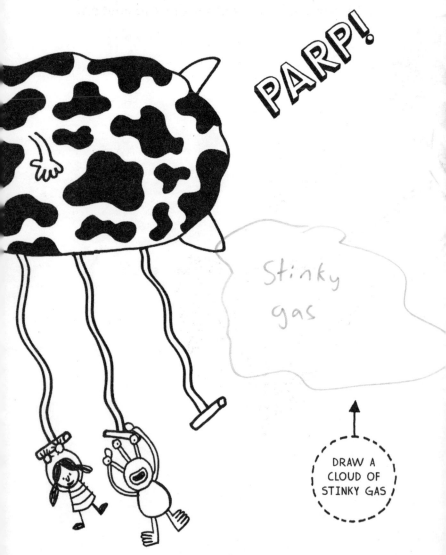

PARP!

Stinky gas

DRAW A CLOUD OF STINKY GAS

It is **SO STINKY** that they all let go of the Gaseous Sprong.

Guess what happens? You got it! They start falling.

Quickly! Draw something soft for them to land on.

At last Daisy, B'ob and Undrawn John have escaped the zoo.

Daisy looks around desperately. "We need to find somewhere to hide."

"Follow me," says B'ob. "I know just the place."

They all run down the street with B'ob leading the way. Suddenly Daisy stops and points to the sky. "Oh no! Look!"

The sky is filled with spaceships! The President's **INVASION FLEET** is launching.

They all stop and stare at the sky in horror.

"What are we going to do?" asks B'ob.

Undrawn John appears to be deep in thought. Or probably would if we could see him. Then he has a **BRILLIANT IDEA!**

"We are going to draw a super-fast spaceship, that's what!"

Draw a **SUPER-FAST** spaceship with some **COOL FINS**, a powerful **ENGINE** and some nice **WING MIRRORS**.

Don't forget to add a **DOOR HANDLE**.

CHAPTER EIGHT
EPIC SPACE BATTLE

With their new **AWESOME** spaceship our heroes
take off in hot pursuit. Soon they are closing in on the
invasion fleet.

"OK," says B'ob. "What's next?"

COLOUR
IN ALL
OF THESE

Guess who has just had **ANOTHER** brilliant idea?
Undrawn John of course! He turns to Daisy and B'ob
with a big grin. "What's the one thing the President
hates the most?"

Of course! **"COLOUR!"**

107

The President is **NOT** impressed. "You've **RUINED** my invasion fleet!"

Look at him. He is having a tantrum, banging his fists on the dashboard. What a big baby.

"I'll get you!" he screams as he starts chasing Daisy and her friends.

He chases them all over space ...

... until eventually he catches up with them.
He squeals with delight. "I have you now!"

But then, just when things look **REALLY BAD**,
a voice shouts over the radio,

"LEAVE THOSE KIDS ALONE!"

Another spaceship drops out of the sky. Look who
it is! It's B'ob's mum!

The President looks over his shoulder in horror.
He is in **BIG TROUBLE** and he knows it.

He holds his breath as Mum takes aim.

ZAPPEWWW!

B'ob's mum zaps the President's spaceship with
loads of **BRIGHT COLOURS**. And we all know how
much he hates bright colours.

COLOUR THE PAGE!

How awesome is B'ob's mum? How awesome are **ALL** mums!

B'ob's mum chases the President right out of the book and then returns to land her spaceship.

A **BIG** crowd has gathered to watch the space battle. And they are all **CHEERING**!

DRAW
MORE
ALIENS

Mum lands to a **HERO'S WELCOME**.

As she gets out of her spaceship, the crowd lifts her up and carries her on their shoulders. They all cheer and wave. They haven't been this happy in a long time.

CHAPTER NINE
MEDALS!

The people of Planet Greyscale decide to award Daisy, John and B'ob with

MEDALS

What do you think the medals should look like?
Oh yeah? That sounds good. Draw the medal.

There is a **BIG PARTY** to celebrate. Our heroes line up to get their reward.

Can you draw the medals around their necks?

Well done! Everyone on Planet Greyscale is delighted, especially the new president ...

It is time for Daisy and Undrawn John to go home.
They leave behind a very different world to the one
they found when they arrived.

Planet Greyscale is going to have to change its name,
I think. Can **YOU** think of an awesome new name?

COLOUR
THE HOUSE

ADD
THE NEW
NAME

WELCOME
TO PLANET

Colour

COLOUR ALL
OF THE
FLOWERS

And soon enough they are back at Planet Scratchpad. Daisy and Undrawn John look out the window at the beautiful world below them. They have never been so happy to see home.

Undrawn John points. "Look. I can see Smile Island."

DRAW
SMILE
ISLAND

B'ob takes them in to land. Below them they can see their **SCHOOL**!

EVERYONE is waiting excitedly for them in the playground.

Miss Scribble is shocked to see Daisy climb out of a spaceship.

"Where have you been, Daisy Doodle?" she asks.

"You are not going to believe this, Miss Scribble," says Daisy.

Everybody listens in **AWE** as Daisy tells the story.

"But I couldn't have done it without the help of one special person," says Daisy. "He is the one person in our class that we should **ALL** pay more attention to."

She is talking, of course, about

UNDRAWN JOHN.

Everyone cheers for Undrawn John. Let's draw him a **HAT** so that everybody will know where he is from now on.

DRAW A HAT ON UNDRAWN JOHN

Now there is only one thing left to do ...

121

THE END

What? You want more?
  OK. Go back to the start and ...

COLOUR IT ALL IN!

How to draw B'ob

1. DRAW THIS SHAPE FOR HIS HEAD

2. DRAW THIS SHAPE FOR HIS BODY

3. DRAW HIS ARMS AND LEGS

4. DRAW GIGANTIC HAIR

BIG GLASSES

DRAW HUGE BIG EARS

GOOFY TEETH

5. See, it's easy! Try it yourself.

Oh dear. You **CRASHED** the spaceship! Well, at least everyone is safe.

Turn to page 72.

THE END

Well, that was silly. Go back to page 68 and have another go.

Remember: **DO NOT PRESS EXPLODE!**

PERMISSION SLIP

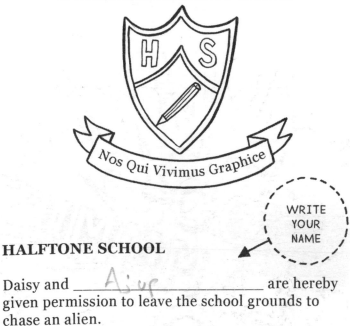

HALFTONE SCHOOL

WRITE YOUR NAME

Daisy and _____ are hereby given permission to leave the school grounds to chase an alien.

Signed: _Principal Rule_

P.s. Make Sure you are back for home time

Tear out this page and remember to **KEEP IT WITH YOU** at all times. Now back to the page you were on.

TEAR PAGE OUT ALONG THIS DOTTED LINE

THE END*

Bye bye!

*Only joking! Go back to page 12.